I MATTER

BY SHIRLITA TILLMAN

I Matter

Publishing assistance provided by TJS Publishing House
www.tjspublishinghouse.com
IG: @tjspublishinghouse
FB: @ tjspublishinghouse

Published in the United States of America

Paperback ISBN-13: 978-0-578-63358-9
Paperback ISBN-10: 0-578-63358-2

DEDICATION

This book is dedicated to ALL boys of color around the world!

ACKNOWLEDGMENTS

This book was inspired by my three kings Jasiah, Jyaire, and Jaden. Without them, this wouldn't have been possible.

Thank you, Kwame Lewis, for sticking behind me and pushing me whenever I have things I want to pursue.

Thank you, Johnetta Luther and J Pics, for all of the videography work.

Thank you to my mother for always pushing me to greatness and for always being my backbone!

To all my sisters that have supported me through my journey, thanks for believing in my vision.

This book is for every boy of color.

It speaks to a child's journey of figuring out their place in this complicated world. It's for all boys and the different feelings they feel in this day and age, where kindness and love are not always shown. This book is *especially* for African American boys who are experiencing being treated differently, no matter how good they are or how well they behave. This book is to empower them and let them know they MATTER.

ONE DAY, I WANT TO BE A DOCTOR.
ONE DAY, I WANT TO BE A LAWYER.
ONE DAY, I WANT TO OWN MY OWN BUSINESS.
COULD I BE THE NEXT PRESIDENT???
I'M A BLACK BOY, AND I MATTER.

1

I WANT TO GO TO COLLEGE.
I WANT TO BE A PART OF THE BAND!
I WANT TO BE AN ENGINEER.

I WONDER WHAT MY FAMILY WILL BE LIKE.
WILL I HAVE KIDS?
WILL MY WIFE BE PRETTY?
I HAVE DREAMS!!!

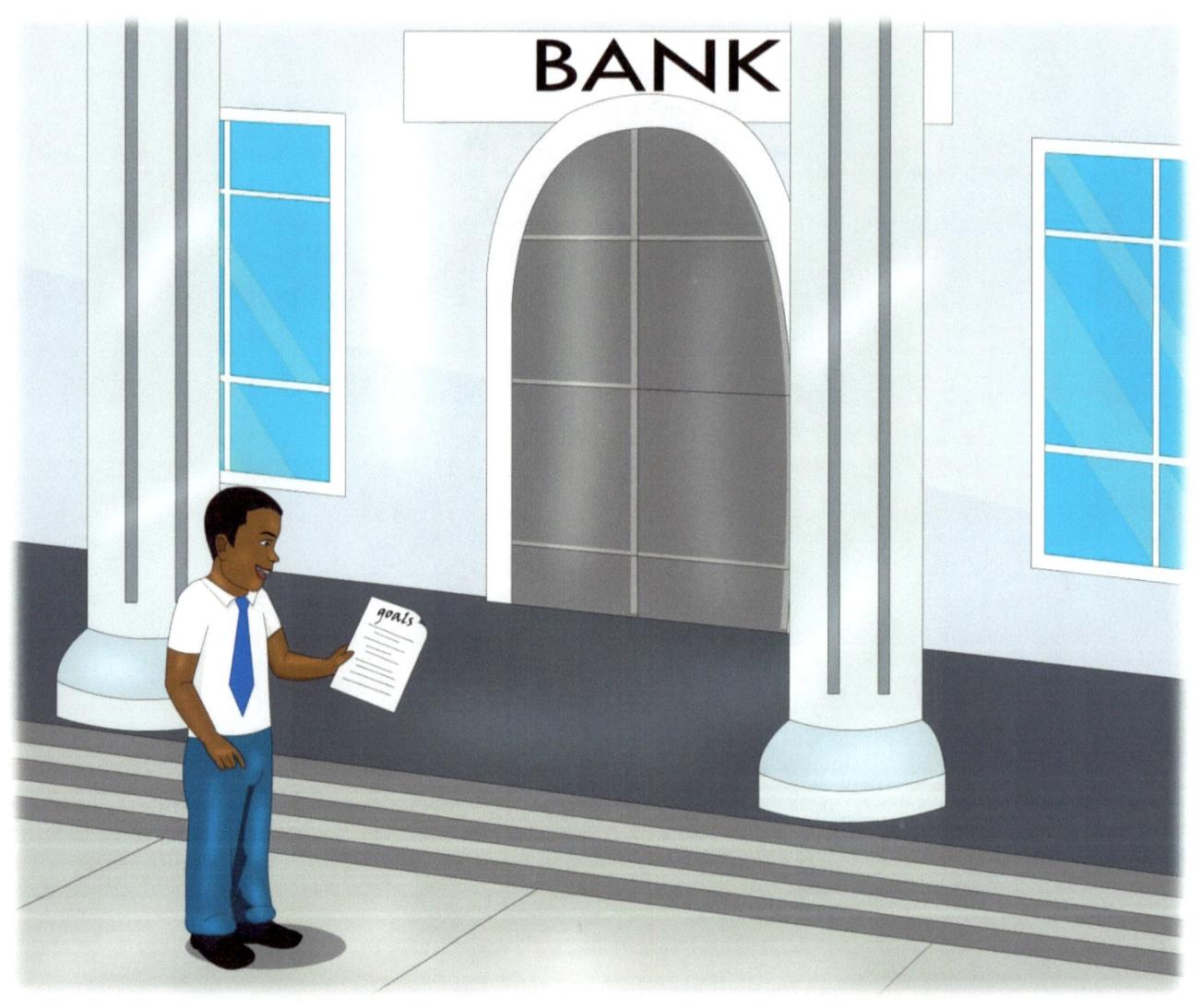

I WANT TO HANG OUT WITH MY FRIENDS WITHOUT WEIRD STARES.
I WANT TO SHOP AND NOT BE FOLLOWED.
BELIEVE IT OR NOT, I'M A YOUNG MAN WITH A JOB!
I HAVE PLANS!!
I'M A BLACK BOY, AND I MATTER.

I'M A BLACK BOY, AND I MATTER!
MY MOM HAS SHOWN ME NOTHING BUT STRENGTH.
I BELIEVE IN MYSELF BECAUSE SHE BELIEVES IN ME.
I WANT TO MAKE HER PROUD.
I AM STRONG.

I HAVE FRIENDS THAT COME IN MANY COLORS,
BUT THEY DON'T HAVE TO DEAL WITH
A LOT OF THE THINGS THAT I DO.
I'M AFRAID TO SEE A POLICE OFFICER.
I USED TO THINK THEY WERE MY FRIEND.
I'M A BLACK BOY, AND I MATTER. RIGHT??

I GO TO CHURCH EVERY SUNDAY.
I MAKE THE HONOR ROLL.
I COLLECT COOL TOY CARS
AND BUILD GIANT TOWERS WITH MY BLOCKS.
I AM A BLACK BOY, AND I MATTER.

I WANT TO WEAR A HOODIE WHEN IT'S COLD
AND NOT BE ACCUSED OF BEING A CRIMINAL.
I JUST WANT THE CHANCE TO LIVE!!
I HAVE FEELINGS!

I MATTER!

I EAT, I SLEEP, AND I READ.

I MAKE MISTAKES, I LEARN, AND I'M INTELLIGENT.

I'M CLEAN, I DRESS NICE, AND I HAVE A HAIRCUT,

I LOVE SCHOOL, I LOVE MY FRIENDS, AND I LOVE MY FAMILY.

I DESERVE A CHANCE AT LIFE.

I DREAM.

I'M STRONG.

I FEEL.

I AM HUMAN.

I'M A BLACK BOY, AND I MATTER!

PLEASE LET ME LIVE!

There is so much more to me than the simple eye can see.

Flaws and all I'm a beautiful soul with dreams and

Aspirations. I have goals. I have plans.

I have friends, and I have a family.

I am a black boy, and I matter.

ABOUT THE AUTHOR

Shirlita Tillman, better known as "Lita" by her close friends and family, is a 32-year-old mother of three boys who are her world. She was recently engaged and is set to marry the love of her life in November of 2020. She is the founder of the women's empowerment group, Ladies with Purpose and Promise, where she connects with women in her community to uplift, empower, and connect them to resources when they are in need.

Anyone who knows Shirlita knows that she is a hard worker and one of the most humble people you'll ever encounter. She is always somewhere smiling, writing, or singing. Shirlita is very passionate about the things she believes in. She is a true inspiration to many. Her hopes are that her work will touch many because it's from such a pure place.